Note to Parents

Look Around!, the Pre-reader level of the *Now I'm Reading!* ™ series, has five stories that are just right for children who want to read, but aren't quite ready to sound out words using phonics. All the stories focus on different but familiar early-learning concepts that are based on the common experiences and interests of young children.

Each story is written with text that follows a sequence of words, which form a pattern. That pattern is then repeated throughout the story with some simple and predictable variations. The colorful illustrations provide visual clues to the text, allowing your child to "read" with increased confidence.

If your child has not yet mastered the recognition of letters and their sounds, you can help introduce him or her to the alphabet through fun-filled activities. For more information on those activities refer to the section on Learning the Alphabet at the end of this book.

NOW I'M READING!™

LOOK AROUND!

PRE-READER ▪ VOLUME 1

Written by Nora Gaydos
Illustrated by BB Sams

Table of Contents

■ STORY 1 ■

COLORS, COLORS

Skills in this story: Recognizing colors; Sight words: *the, is, of*

The flower is red.

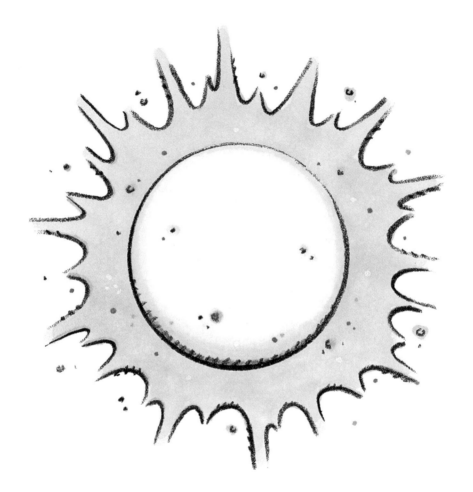

The sun is yellow.

The frog is green.

The plum is purple.

The bird is blue.

The carrot is orange.

The pig is pink.

The bear is brown.

The bat is black.

The rainbow is full of colors!

TEN SCOOPS

Skills in this story: Counting to ten; Sight words: *I, have, on, the*

I have one scoop on the cone.

I have two scoops on the cone.

I have three scoops on the cone.

I have four scoops on the cone.

I have five scoops on the cone.

I have six scoops on the cone.

I have seven scoops on the cone.

I have eight scoops on the cone.

I have nine scoops on the cone.

I have ten scoops on the ground!

FUNNY FACES

Skills in this story: Recognizing different feelings; Sight words: *I, see, a, of*

I see a happy face.

I see a sad face.

I see a scared face.

I see a mad face.

I see a shy face.

I see a surprised face.

I see a proud face.

I see a sorry face.

I see a sleepy face.

I see lots of funny faces.

I LIKE TO EAT!

Skills in this story: Recognizing different foods; Sight words: *I, like, to*

I like to eat tomatoes.

I like to eat cheese.

I like to eat pepperoni.

I like to eat green peppers.

I like to eat onions.

I like to eat meatballs.

I like to eat mushrooms.

I like to eat olives.

I like to eat bread.

I like to eat pizza!

TOO MANY PETS

Skills in this story: Recognizing common pets; Sight words: *I, have, a, in, my, too*

I have a pet dog in my house.

I have a pet cat in my house.

I have a pet hamster in my house.

I have a pet bird in my house.

I have a pet fish in my house.

I have a pet rabbit in my house.

I have a pet snake in my house.

I have a pet frog in my house.

I have a pet lizard in my house.

I have too many pets in my house!

How to Use This Book

Prepare by reading the stories ahead of time.
Familiarize yourself with the sight words and the concept-related words in each story. In doing this, you can better guide your child to recognize those words in the text.

Discuss each early learning concept. Before reading, look at a story's title page with your child. Talk about the concept and how it relates to your child's own world. Ask your child what he or she knows about the topic. Encourage him or her to make predictions about what the story will be about.

Read each story aloud to your child. Invite your child to look at the pictures as you read the words in the story. To promote a connection between the spoken word and the printed word, point to the words as you read. Point out the repetitive word pattern that appears in each story.

Read each story with your child. Have your child join in and read along with you. Your child will naturally pick up on the patterned, repetitive text in each story.

Have your child "read" to you. Encourage your child to use the picture clues and to point to the words as he or she "reads."

Sound out the beginning letters of words. After your child is familiar with the patterned text, focus on the sounds and letters in different words. This will help create a natural bridge to the next step in reading—using phonics.

Glossary of Terms

Emergent Literacy: An early stage in the development of "conventional literacy" in which children explore and develop the various skills involved in reading and writing.

Consonant Letters: Letters that represent the consonant sounds and, except for *Y*, are not vowels—*B, C, D, F, G, H, J, K, L, M, N, P, Q, R, S, T, V, W, X, Y, Z.*

Decoding: Breaking a word into parts, giving each letter or letter combination its corresponding sound, and then pronouncing the word (sometimes called "sounding out").

Sight Words: Frequently used words, recognized automatically on sight, which do not require decoding (such as *a, the, is* and so on).

Visual Clues: Distinctive pictures that readers can use to help them identify an unknown word.

Patterned, Repetitive Text: Text that follows a specific sequence or pattern and is repeated throughout the book (such as—*I like red.; I like blue.; I like pink.*).

Learning the Alphabet

Children learn best when the learning is meaningful and engaging. Help your child discover the letters and sounds that are all around, so he or she can attach meaning and importance to the task of learning the alphabet.

- **Immerse your child in alphabet-rich surroundings:**
  1. Sing alphabet songs.
  2. Read alphabet books and poems.
  3. Display an alphabet strip somewhere in the house.
  4. Practice writing letters using finger paint.

- **Use environmental print with your child:** Environmental print is the print we see all around us on commercial signs, billboards, and labels. It's the first print a child recognizes. Encourage your child to identify letters on signs at different places.

- **Make an A-B-C scrapbook:** Get a blank scrapbook and title each page with an alphabet letter. Using your favorite advertisements, food labels, logos, and so on, cut out and glue an example on each page of the alphabet book to promote an association between the letters and the sounds.

The Now I'm Reading!™ Series

The *Now I'm Reading!*™ series integrates the best of phonics and literature-based reading. Phonics emphasizes letter-sound relationships, while a literature-based approach brings the enjoyment and excitement of a real story. The series has six reading levels:

Pre-Reader level: Children "read" simple, patterned, and repetitive text, and use picture clues to help them along.

Level 1: Children learn short vowel sounds, simple consonant sounds, and common sight words.

Level 2: Children learn long and short vowel sounds, more consonants and consonant blends, plus more sight word reinforcement.

Level 3: Children learn new vowel sounds, with more consonant blends, double consonants, and longer words and sentences.

Level 4: Children learn advanced word skills, including silent letters, multi-syllable words, compound words, and contractions.

Independent level: Children are introduced to high-interest topics as they tackle challenging vocabulary words and information by using previous phonics skills.

About the Author

Nora Gaydos is an elementary school teacher with more than ten years of classroom experience teaching kindergarten, first grade, and third grade. She has a broad understanding of how beginning readers develop from the earliest stage of pre-reading to becoming independent, self-motivated readers. Nora has a degree in elementary education from Miami University in Ohio and lives in Connecticut with her husband and two sons. Nora is also the author of *Now I Know My ABCs* and *Now I Know My 1, 2, 3's*, as well as other early-learning concept books published by innovative KIDS®.